For Mum and Dad and Simon

With thanks to Paddington Pooka
for her example and assistance

First published 1988 by
Walker Books Ltd, 87 Vauxhall Walk
London SE11 5HJ

© 1988 Penny Dale

This edition published 1990
Reprinted 1991, 1993

Printed and bound in Hong Kong by
Sheck Wah Tong Printing Press Ltd

British Library Cataloguing in Publication Data
A catalogue record for this book is
available from the British Library.
ISBN 0-7445-1467-3

Wake Up Mr. B!

Penny Dale

WALKER BOOKS
LONDON

Rosie woke up very early.

She went to wake up Billy.

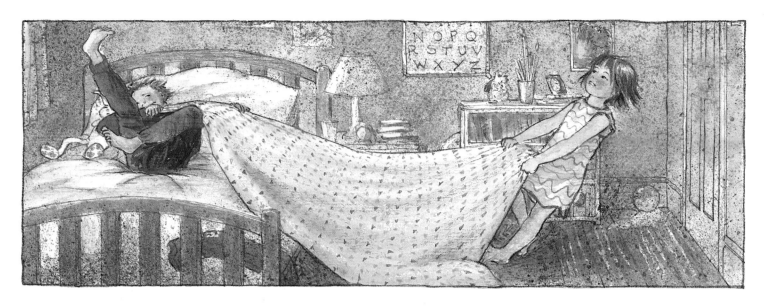

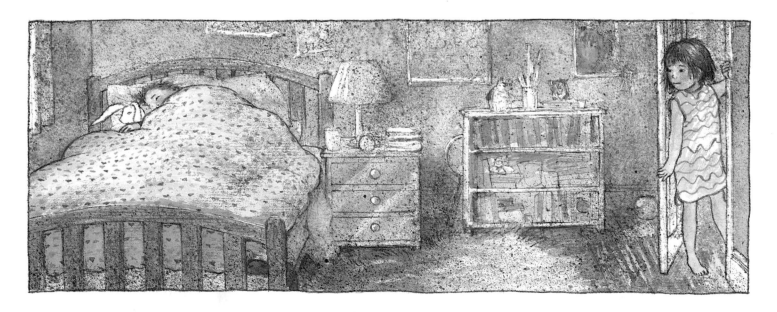

She went to wake up Dad.

She went to find Mr. B.

"Wake up, Mr. B," she said.

"Come with me, Mr. B," she said.

"Let's get dressed."

"Get in my car, Mr. B," she said.

"We're driving to the sea."

"Get in my boat, Mr. B," she said.

"We're sailing round the world."

"Get in my balloon, Mr. B," she said.

"Don't fall asleep. We're flying to the moon."

"Come and see Rosie and Mr. B," said Billy.

"Wake up, Rosie! Wake up, Mr. B!"